SUPERWORM

By Julia Donaldson

Illustrated by Axel Scheffler

Arthur A. Levine Books
An Imprint of Scholastic Inc.

Superworm is super-long.
Superworm is super-strong.
Watch him wiggle! See him squirm!
Hip, hip, hooray for SUPERWORM!

Help! Disaster! Baby toad
Has hopped onto a major road.

"Someone help him! Quick! Oh no!"

Look — a SUPERWORM lasso!

The bees are feeling bored today.
They need a nice new game to play.
Cheer up, bees! No need to mope . . .

It's SUPERWORM, the skipping rope!

Beetle's fallen in the well!
Is she drowning? Who can tell?

Not to panic — all is fine . . .

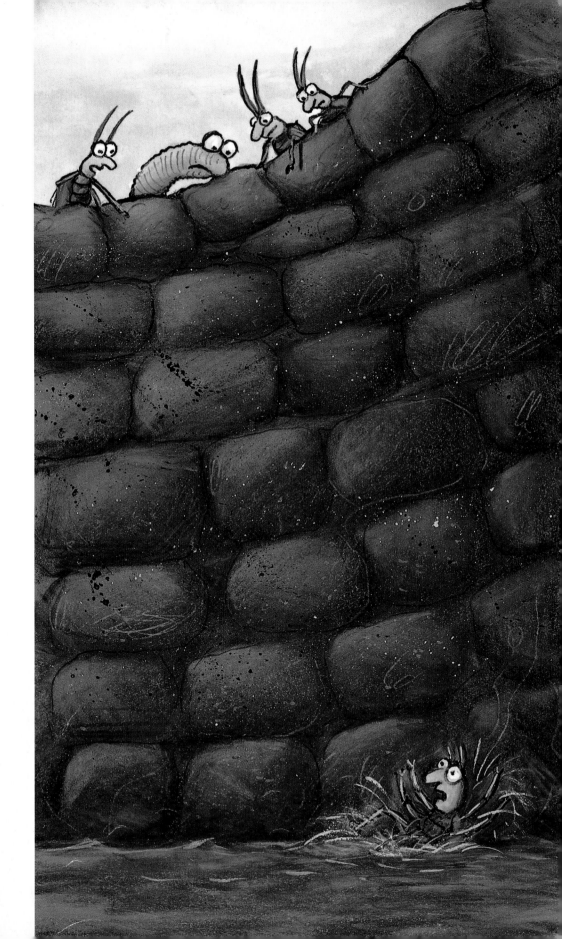

It's SUPERWORM, the fishing line!

Then toads and beetles, bees and bugs,
Brother snails and sister slugs,
Uncle earwig, auntie ant
Clap and cheer and chant this chant:

"Superworm is super-long.
Superworm is super-strong.
Watch him wiggle! See him squirm!
Hip, hip, hooray for SUPERWORM!"

The chant is carried on the air
To Wizard Lizard in his lair.
He mutters in his servant's ear,
"Find that worm and bring him here."

The servant crow is black and grim.

Everyone is scared of him.

They all let out a fearful shriek

To see their hero in his beak.

The wizard waves his magic flower.
"Now, Superworm, you're in my power
And you must tunnel, writhe, and coil,
To find me treasure in the soil."

Superworm is very cross
To have a lizard as his boss,
But when he tries to slink away
The wizard's magic makes him stay.

For days he tunnels, twists, and winds,
But all the treasure that he finds
Is two small buttons, half a cork,
A toffee, and a plastic fork.

The lizard flicks an angry tail.
"Have one last try, and if you fail
To find that treasure down below,
I'll feed you to my hungry crow."

The crow is flapping
    through the night.
Everyone looks up in fright.
They see him perch upon an oak
And listen to his dreadful croak:

"Superworm is good to eat!
Superworm's a special treat!
He'll be juicy, fat, and firm.
Hip, hip, hooray
    for SUPERWORM!"

"Action! Quickly! At the double!
Superworm's in frightful trouble!
We must help him if we can.
We must hatch a cunning plan!"

The garden creatures leave their home,
Carrying a honeycomb.
They jump and fly and crawl and creep . . .

. . . and find the lizard fast asleep.

They chew the petals off his flower
To rob him of his magic power.

The caterpillars fetch some leaves,

While busily the spider weaves.

The web is strong. The web is tough.
The web is plenty big enough.

The wizard wakes. "This isn't funny!
I'm wrapped in leaves and stuck with honey!"

Then up the bees and beetles fly
And lift the web into the sky.

"This is the place!" and . . .

BANG! CRASH! THUMP!
The wizard's in the rubbish dump!

And now, from somewhere underground
There comes a distant rumbling sound.
The earth begins to heave, and then . . .

... SUPERWORM is back again!

Superworm, the swing!

The slide!

The hula hoop!

The fairground ride!

Then toads and beetles, bees and bugs,
Brother snails and sister slugs,
Uncle earwig, auntie ant
Clap and cheer and chant this chant:

"Superworm is super-long.
Superworm is super-strong.
Watch him wiggle! See him squirm!
Hip, hip, hooray for SUPERWORM!"

For Leo

Library of Congress Cataloging-in-Publication Data
Donaldson, Julia.
Superworm / by Julia Donaldson ; illustrated by Axel Scheffler. — First American edition.
pages cm
Summary: Superworm's bug friends attempt to free him from the clutches of Wizard Lizard
who, having heard of Superworm's wondrous and heroic deeds, captures him and forces him
to dig for treasure. • ISBN 978-0-545-59176-8 (hardcover : alk. paper) [1. Stories in
rhyme. 2. Worms — Fiction. 3. Heroes — Fiction. 4. Insects — Fiction. 5. Wizards —
Fiction. 6. Lizards — Fiction.] I. Scheffler, Axel, illustrator.
II. Title. • PZ8.3.D7235Sup 2014h • [E] — dc23 • 2013001546

10 9 8 7 6 5 4   16 17 18

Printed in Malaysia

First American edition, February 2014